Lee Aucoin, *Creative Director*
Jamey Acosta, *Senior Editor*
Heidi Fiedler, *Editor*
Produced and designed by
Denise Ryan & Associates
Illustration © Sophie Kittredge
Rachelle Cracchiolo, *Publisher*

Teacher Created Materials

5301 Oceanus Drive
Huntington Beach, CA 92649-1030
http://www.tcmpub.com
Paperback: ISBN: 978-1-4333-5559-2
Library Binding: ISBN: 978-1-4807-1704-6

The Lonely Penguin's Blog

Written by Alan Trussell-Cullen

Illustrated by Sophie Kittredge

Penguin Blog

June 15: Hello, World!

Welcome to my blog. This is me, Palaki, and I'm a three-year-old emperor penguin. I have been on a long swim north to see the world. Now, I'm finally heading south to my home in the freezing cold waters off Antarctica.

3

Penguin Blog

June 17: Something is wrong!

The sea water should be getting colder as I swim south, but it is getting warmer. *Am I lost, I wonder. Am I swimming the wrong way?*

Penguin Blog

June 18: Any Icebergs?

I keep looking for icebergs! I'm looking for leopard seals, too. They love to eat penguins. I've got to watch out for orcas, too!

Penguin Blog

June 20: I'm in Big Trouble!

I was swimming along when I saw something white ahead. I thought it was ice and I was home at last. I swam straight for it, but look where I ended up!

9

Penguin Blog

June 21: Where Am I?

People keep looking at me and taking photos. They say this is Peka Peka Beach and I'm in New Zealand. I'm the first emperor penguin to come here in 44 years! That means I'm nearly 2,000 miles away from home!

AUSTRALIA

ZOO

Peka Peka Beach
Wellington

NEW ZEALAND

South Pacific Ocean

ANTARCTICA

11

Penguin Blog

June 22: My Big Mistake

When we get thirsty in Antarctica, we swallow some white snow, so I tried swallowing some of the white stuff on the beach. Yuck! It tasted awful!

13

Penguin Blog

June 23: I Feel Sick!

My stomach hurts so much and I think it's from all that white stuff I ate! I'm worried. The people are worried, too.

Penguin Blog

June 24: Wellington Zoo

The people decided I needed help. They've taken me to Wellington Zoo. They made this special room for me. It's very cold. They even made a bed of ice for me to sleep on.

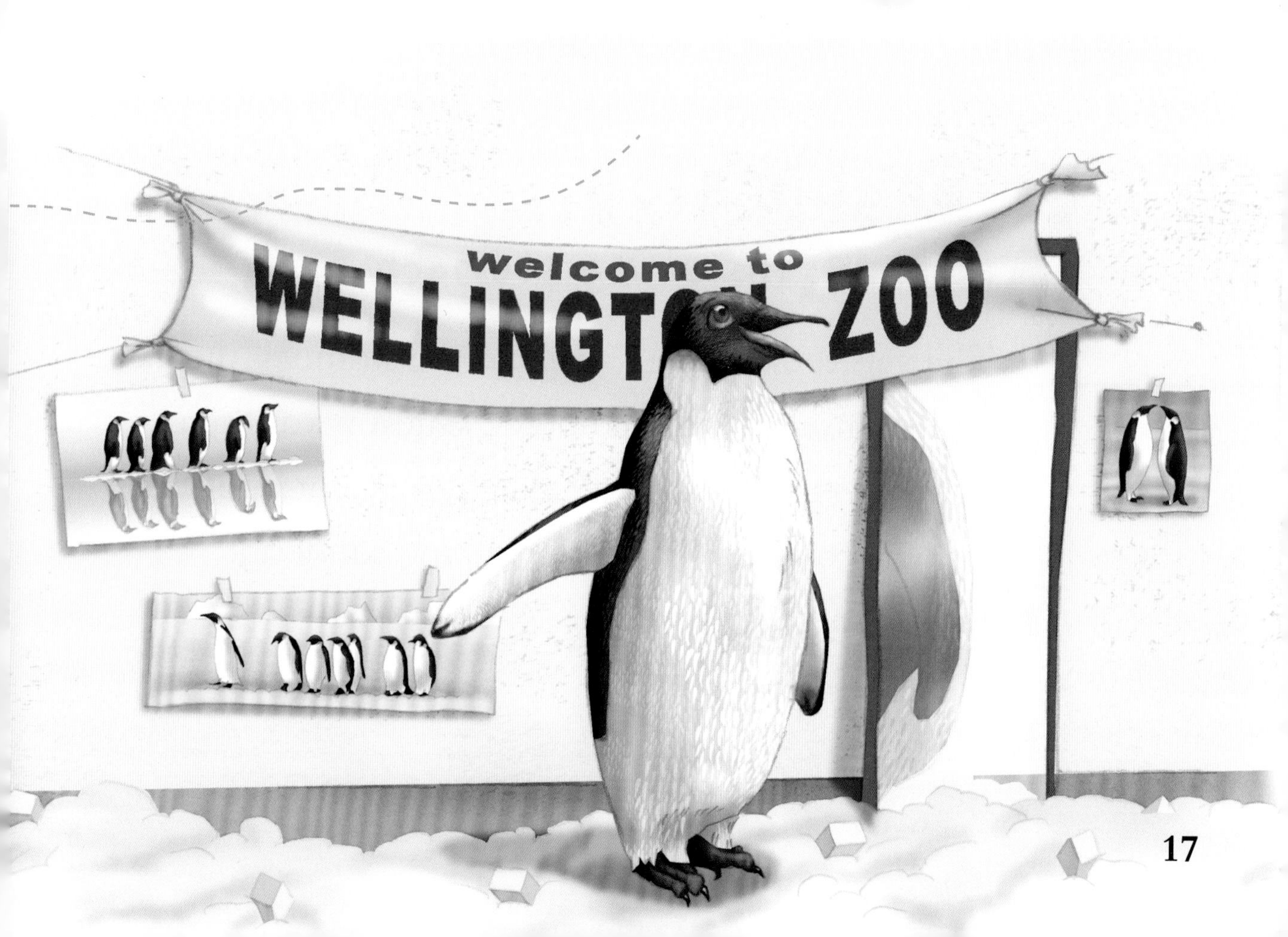
welcome to
WELLINGTO
ZOO

Penguin Blog

June 28: Inside My Stomach

The vets took some X-rays of my stomach and looked inside with a camera. Guess what they found? Sand. Lots of it! They took out about a pound of sand! I was a walking sandbag! I'm feeling better now.

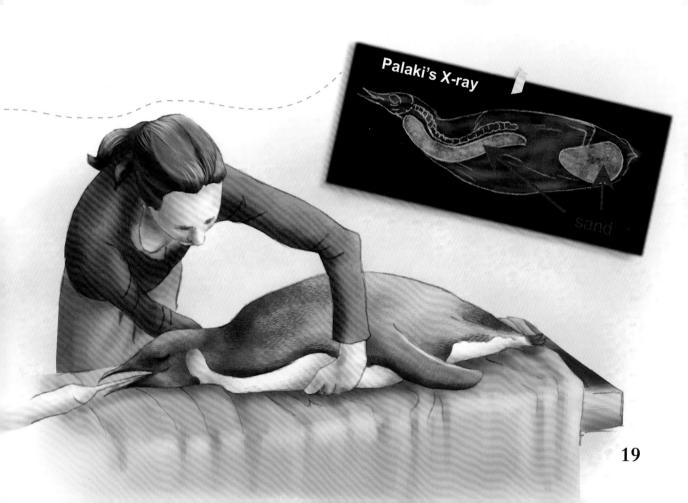

Palaki's X-ray

sand

Penguin Blog

July 25: Snow!

Today was the coldest day Wellington has ever had. It even snowed! That hardly ever happens here. It was so cold they let me swim in a pool outside. It was wonderful!

Penguin Blog

August 19: Getting Ready to Go Home

I'm getting strong now. The vets at the zoo think it's time for me to swim back home. They are going to take me half way in a ship and let me swim the rest. I can't wait.

Penguin Blog

August 28: Testing! Testing!

Today, they fixed this transmitter to my feathers. It will send out signals so people know where I am when I am swimming. I hope it stays put!

Penguin Blog

August 29: All Aboard!

They took me to the ship in a special crate. The ship is called the *Tangaroa*. The people were sad to see me go. We've been sailing for days and now it's time for my big swim. They made this ramp for me to slide down. Everyone said goodbye. Then, I was swimming in the sea. It was wonderful.

Penguin Blog

September 8: Time to Say Goodbye.

I am swimming well, but the transmitter came off today. Too bad! The water is getting colder every day so I must be swimming in the right direction. Soon, I will see ice floating on the water and other emperor penguins. That's when I will know I am home. This will be my last penguin blog. This is Palaki signing off. Thanks for your help. Goodbye!